NOTES FROM A

Broken

Heart

Things I Wanted To Say

By

Elaine Wills, M.Ed.

Eyegate Inspirations and Publishing

eyegatepublishing@yahoo.com

ISBN: 978-1-7366801-1-7

willselaine2010@yahoo.com

Realistic Fiction

DEDICATION

Notes from a broken heart is dedicated to anyone left brokenhearted because an uncaring, inconsiderate lover ended the relationship without allowing closure. This book contains intimate thoughts of a scorned lover. Things she wanted to say, and her private thoughts are documented as she attempted to express the depth of her despair.

ACKNOWLEDGMENTS

Without God, I am nothing. Mayme L. Harris, my beloved mother, encouraged me to dream, and my father, Willie Walker Jr., taught me to think for myself. My sons Damon, Edward, Charles, and my grandson CJ are the jewels in my crown. Thank you for believing in me to my friends and family who put up with my random brainstorming.

Contents

Prologue

Things occur in life that trigger the darker side of our private thoughts. How do you grieve an unrequited relationship or mourn a lost love? What does it take to get over a lover who leaves without explanation or notice, tearing your heart to pieces? What about the person who wronged you and ignores you as if it were you that did something to him or her? She or he refuses to answer your calls or talk face to face. The former partner treats you like you are dead to her or him, while she or he is very much alive to you. Death would be easier to cope with; at least there is a body to bury. You might as well be dead. The impact of what happens in the heart of someone who falls in love with the uncaring person can be devastating. Does the perpetrator get to walk away with no consequence? The answer is yes, they do.

How many times have you felt a deep love connection with someone and wondered if the person felt it too? How do you deal with that situation? Do you play it safe and say nothing or assist that person by making yourself useful in some aspect of his or her life, hoping to get noticed? Do you risk rejection by voicing your feelings on the off chance that the one you love and admire will reciprocate? Either way, you leave yourself vulnerable. Love is a gamble that does not feel good to lose under any circumstance.

Notes from a Broken Heart is about a woman who bet on love and lost. She fell in love with a man that did not love her. The notes in this book reflect her effort to regain control of her life and emotions through written expression. She had no outlet for her pain and was too embarrassed and humiliated to tell anyone what happened, so she wrote her truth.

Sirrah had a good life. She was successful and financially stable, but something was missing. She didn't have a mate.

She longed for the kind of love that she witnessed between her mother and father. They had the sparkle of love. Sirrah met Bennie Zoudiki and trusted him to fill the void. She gave him the best of herself in anticipation of becoming his wife. For five years, Sirrah opened her heart and her finances to his promise of marriage. The more she gave, the farther away the promise moved. Sirrah put her hope and faith in a man. She put Bennie before her family. Most importantly, she put a man before God.

Notes from a Broken Heart is Sirrah's reaction to the relationship with a man who almost took everything from her. Not only did he break Sirrah's heart and cause financial damage, he also took peace of mind and damaged her spirit. The relationship brought her to a point where she wanted to die. Sirrah's notes began as a suicide letter, pointing blame at the person who hurt her. She wanted everyone to know what Bennie did, how he treated her with disdain while she treasured and adored him. Bennie led her down a rabbit hole where nothing was real like *Alice's Adventures in Wonderland*. She was left to figure out if he ever really loved her. Sirrah took care of his personal and physical needs. Casting her pearls before swine, she assumed a wife's duties without the benefit of being a wife. She loaned or ultimately gave him money because he never paid her back. Sirrah couldn't prove it wasn't an act of love after loaning Bennie cash because he wouldn't sign a promissory note. He questioned her trust when she brought it up. Sirrah thought they were in a loving relationship, especially when Bennie proposed and moved into her house. He pulled her into a false sense of security with promises of a bright future together. She allowed him access to everything, including her body, and all he did was take what she offered. Sirrah would later see the rift between his words and his actions. She mistook his actions for love. It was all a lie.

Chapter 1

Sirrah Noel Washington was the seventeen-year-old only child of Zahara and Nicholas Washington. Zahara, a freelance restoration artist, is African American, and her father, Nicholas, is Caucasian. Nicholas, a colonel in the Air Force, was commander in charge of all training at the flight test center. Flying was his passion. They lived on Edwards Air Force Base, called the middle of nowhere because it was in the Mojave Desert. It was an exciting place for Sirrah to grow up. It allowed easy access to areas with different climates. Her family visited Mammoth Mountain to ski. Las Vegas was four hours away, and Los Angeles was two hours in the opposite direction if they wanted to visit the beach. The Air Force base regularly provided entertainment. Sirrah thought the base's most exciting feature was its flight test center. She loved watching different aircraft take-off and witnessed the Space Shuttle Columbia land in the lake bed.

Sirrah knew her parents loved and adored her. Her father encouraged her to be a strong Black woman. Even though she is biracial, he knew society would view his daughter as a Black woman. Nicholas was persistent in telling her she could be whatever she wanted and to not limit herself to mediocracy. Sirrah had a strong sense of self-worth and the value she represents as a person. Sirrah never doubted it when her parents told her that she was strong and beautiful and that the world was hers to explore. They believed women and men should abstain from sex before marriage, so much so that Sirrah signed a contract agreeing to remain a virgin until she was married. It was easy to get Sirrah to sign because it came with a beautiful diamond promise ring as a reminder of her commitment to God. Sirrah's parents agreed that Sirrah should travel with her mother during her frequent freelance assignments to show Sirrah that hardworking African

American women can achieve great things. Zahara was a staunch advocate for human rights and encouraged Sirrah to be an independent thinker.

Zahara homeschooled Sirrah until the eleventh grade. The curriculum was more advanced than in public schools. She had tutors for academic subjects and participated in after-school sports and extracurricular activities offered through Desert High School, located on the base. Sirrah's social circle was limited to other teens who lived on the base. She had many acquaintances, but she had not developed close friendships with the other military families because of frequent travels with her mother. The kids on the base had social cliques, and Sirrah wasn't around them enough to belong.

Sirrah's father was an only child, born in Alabama. He and his parents were estranged. He did not have a close bond with any of his relatives. They shunned and disinherited him because of his marriage to a Black woman. His father refused even to say his name. Sirrah's mother frequently teased, saying they are mad because a black woman stole their family's crown jewel. Nicholas was the only one who graduated from college and an officer in the Air Force. They had high hopes for him until Zahara came along. They acted as if marrying outside of his race diminished his worth. Nicholas said it's their problem if a racial conflict prevented them from knowing the most spectacular woman in the world. Zahara's mother, Mina, accepted Nicholas and loved him as if he was her son. Zahara and Nicholas were best friends. Sirrah's parents were always kissing and hugging. Their eyes beamed with joy when they saw each other, or they would giggle over the phone when they were apart. They were inseparable when they were not working. They were a perfect match.

Sirrah's mother, Zahara, was a native Detroiter. She had strong family ties and stayed in contact with her family. No matter where she went, she called her mother to check-in every other day. She had three brothers and two sisters. Sirrah loved visiting her maternal grandmother Mina in Detroit, where most of her mother's family still lived. Sirrah stayed with Grandmother Mina for a month every summer since she was a little girl. Sirrah bragged about being from Detroit, thinking big- city ties gave her cool points with the other teens who lived on the Air Force Base. Her cousins teased her, saying she was a valley girl gangster. Sirrah was always ready for a challenge and eager to try new things. Detroit was a new and exciting place compared to the Edwards Air Force Base. She was mesmerized by the fast-paced city life and the idea of catching a city bus. There were no busses or transit systems in the desert. She wanted to ride all of them to see where they went. One would think she was on a ride at an amusement park. Even though they called her crazy for wanting to ride buses all day, her cousins were her best friends. She socialized, partied, and went to dances with them. They regularly communicated through social media and over the phone. Sirrah always had a great time when she visited Detroit.

To Sirrah, going to Grandma Mina's house was like going to the park. Grandmother Mina lived in a five-bedroom house with a huge lot. She had a picnic area with a brick barbecue grill, a swing, a jungle gym set, and a basketball court for her grandchildren. She installed a ten-foot stockade fence for privacy and noise control as a courtesy to her neighbors. Her house was a gathering place for everybody. The children often had basketball competitions to show off their basketball skills to the family. They all enjoyed playing or watching basketball. Sunday dinner was always at Grandmother Mina's house.

Sirrah's favorite cousin Johnny B loved to play basketball. He would say, "My name is Johnny, and the *B* is for basketball. Johnny B was the whole package because he was also a mathematics whizz. He could figure out mathematics problems in his head and quickly give the correct answers. Sirrah called him a double threat, a jock with brains. Although he loves basketball, he ultimately wanted to be an engineer. She practiced so often with him that she also became an excellent ball player.

Sirrah and Johnny B were inseparable when she visited Detroit. She enjoyed playing basketball because of Johnny B. She was an exceptional ball player, but it wasn't her passion. They would team up challenge other ball players in *twenty-one*, which the first team to score twenty-one points wins. Johnny B made bets because opponents were overconfident that they could beat him with Sirrah as his teammate. Their opponents would get mad when they lost to a girl. To make matters worse, she would get in their face calling them little boys to throw them off their game. One guy had to shave his head because he lost to Sirrah.

Johnny B nicknamed her Goddess Sirrah because God gave her exceptional basketball skills. Sirrah's had a perfect jump shot. She could hit a three-pointer from anywhere on the court. Everyone called her Goddess Sirrah once they heard it from Johnny B. The name fit her in more ways than one. Standing a statuesque 5 feet and 9 inches tall, Sirrah was athletic but feminine with muscles and a six-pack. Sirrah was the baddest chick on the basketball court and always dressed to impress off the court. She had blue eyes, a narrow nose, and full lips. Sirrah knew that people pay for lip injections to get her lips. She was light brown with natural flecks of golden blond in her hair. Sirrah wore her curly hair in a short bob cut. Longer hair only got in her way when she was playing ball. In the summer, she would tan to a golden brown. The golden highlights in her hair made her look like a sun goddess.

Chapter 2

Life dealt Sirrah and her mother, Zahara, a harsh blow. Nicholas was killed in a helicopter crash during a training maneuver three months before Sirrah graduated high school. He received a military burial with honors. Zahara was devastated. They planned to retire and spend time getting reacquainted as husband and wife after Sirrah graduated. Sirrah planned to travel abroad for a year before going to college. That all changed after her father died. He was the apple of her eyes. Due to the severity of the helicopter crash, they never saw his body. He went to work one day and never came home. It was challenging to come to grips with his death. There was no real closure for Sirrah. Her dad was just gone. She wanted to stay close to her mother.

Nicholas was Zahara's only love. In her eyes, no one would ever fill his shoes. The years of happiness with him were all she ever wanted and more than she ever dreamed. Zahara vowed never to remarry. Zahara was alone but not lonely. They stayed on the base until Sirrah graduated as a courtesy to the memory of Nicholas. Edwards Air Force Base was the only home Sirrah had ever known. They couldn't permanently live on the base because there was no longer an active service member in the family. Zahara moved to Detroit and formed a nonprofit organization to honor her late husband. Nicholas had a lucrative accidental death policy. He left three million dollars to his wife and two million to his daughter, in addition to his military beneficiary policy. He always said he would provide for them even in death. Nicholas kept his word.

Zahara kept busy to lessen the impact of losing her husband, while at the same time, she was emotionally disconnecting from Sirrah. Sirrah felt lost without her father.

Knowing that no one would ever replace her father, she experienced a deep sense of helplessness as she grieved. Sirrah was in awe of her mother's resilience. Zahara said her faith in God was the only thing she had to lean on. Sirrah was by her side, praying for comfort. Zahara showed extraordinary strength handling the burial, the relocation, and organizing the Nocholas Washington Foundation in remembrance of Sirrah's father.

There were awkward times for Sirrah and her mother. They both threw themselves into their passions, trying not to be a burden to one another. Her father's death created a distance between them that unintentionally evolved. They rarely had dinner together anymore, except for Sunday dinner at Grandmother Mina's. Zahara stopped asking Sirrah about her day or how she was doing and left money on the counter for Sirrah with notes telling her where she would be for the day and how to reach her. That was the extent of their communication. Sirrah was happy the relocation to Detroit put her closer to her grandmother. Her mother needed more support than Sirrah knew how to give. Grandmother Mina would know what to do for her daughter Zahara. Sirrah had a praying grandmother, who taught her that trusting in God was the answer to overcoming any obstacle or healing any hurt. Sirrah often prayed to relieve the pain of her father's passing and the loss of emotional attachment with her mother.

Johnny B was there to comfort Sirrah through her grief. He never left her side when she arrived in Detroit. He did everything in his power to encourage her and lift her spirits. Sirrah went to practice with Johnny B to keep him from missing practice trying to console her. She met Cindy Perry, the head coach for U of D's women's basketball team, while playing ball with Johnny B before practice. Johnny B bragged about his cousin Goddess Sirrah so often; the coach already knew who she was. Coach Perry thought her first name was *Goddess*, and her last name was *Sirrah*. Sirrah was in the gym so much, the coach noticed her skills and suggested that Sirrah tryout for the women's basketball team. She was not taking the suggestion seriously until Johnny B dared her. He tapped into her competitive nature. Goddess Sirrah never passed on a challenge. She showed up to tryouts and showed off her jump shot and defensive skills. Coach Perry said Sirrah would be a great asset to her team. She expedited her admission to the school and allocated money for a full scholarship. Sirrah could not believe her luck. She didn't need the scholarship, but it felt like she won the lottery. U of

D was a prestigious school, and she didn't have to worry about leaving her mother alone so soon after her father's death. God worked it out. Her mother was beaming with pride when Sirrah told her the news. Zahara took the whole family to their favorite restaurant.

Sirrah and Johnny B became closer than ever. They were cousins, best friends, and now they were going to school together. Sirrah's teammates became her extended family. She was with teammates when she was not with Johnny B or at home. Goddess Sirrah was becoming well known on and off the court. She still challenged her cousin on and off the court because that's what he loved. Life was good.

Once school started, girls approached Sirrah for information about Johnny B, attempting to convince her to put a good word for them, and guys questioned Johnny B about Sirrah. They were popular in their community. Not wanting to spoil their reputations, they were mindful of their associations. They had a strict upbringing. Fornication or sex of any kind outside of marriage was frowned upon by their family. Grandmother Mina said, "Keep your pants up and your legs crossed." Johnny was not a playboy because of this.

Sirrah's first year of college passed quickly. After studying and basketball practice, she didn't have time to socialize. However, Johnny B fell in love with something other than basketball. He met Simone at acampus party. She was a pre-med student. Simone lived on campus, and Johnny started spending nights with her. Sirrah was happy that he picked love over basketball. She teased him for being mushy over a girl like she did when they were children. Johnny missed several Sunday dinners, and his mother, Auntie Rena, was not pleased. She questioned Sirrah about what Johnny was doing and why he wasn't coming to dinner. Sirrah felt caught in the middle, having to explain why he was not coming home. She convinced Johnny B to tell his mother about his girlfriend.

Johnny B handled his business by bringing Simone to meet the family. She was a sweet person with goals and ambitions that fit well with their expectations. They were a good match. The couple may as well start planning their wedding. Johnny B dodged a bullet. That prompted Grandmother Mina to ask Sirrah when she was bringing a boyfriend home. Sirrah jokingly responded, "You know I ain't got time for that." Grandmother Mina shook her head and laughed. Sirrah would laugh when Grandma Mina nagged her about getting a husband and giving her great-grandchildren.

Chapter 3

Sirrah met Bennie when she was tutoring disadvantaged youth at the Collingwood Boys and Girls Club. U of D requires sophomores to do community service as part of their scholarship obligation. Sirrah chose to volunteer at the Boys and Girls Club, where Johnny B practiced as a kid. She tutored for ten hours a week. The Boys and Girls Club is where she crossed paths with Bennie Zoudiki.

Bennie was also a volunteer. He approached her in the parking lot to tell her that he was a fan. Surprised that he knew she played ball, she asked, "Do I know you?" The tone of her response was not friendly. Bennie explained he went to all the games at U of D, including women's basketball. That's how he recognized her. She didn't like being approached by strangers, but she adjusted her attitude after his explanation. Bennie looked seven feet tall. He had dark chocolate skin, and his teeth were pearly white. The contrast between his teeth and his skin was a contradiction. His face was proof that dark and light can occupy the same space. His eye color was so dark they looked bluish. He reminded her of Manute Bol in height, with Dominique Wilkins's face. He was handsome. She politely said, "Thank you," with a sarcastic smirk. She walked away, wondering if he could play basketball.

Bennie continued to follow her to her car. Abruptly turning to him, she asked, "Are you following me?" Bennie stopped in his tracks, nervously responding that he walked female volunteers to their vehicles as a courtesy and meant no harm. Sirrah arrogantly told him, "I don't need protecting," and thanked him for the effort. He looked confused and continued to follow her as if he didn't hear her. She figured he was fresh off the boat and didn't understand what she said. She politely thanked him and got into her car. Bennie stood in one spot, watching Sirrah leave the parking lot. "That was strange," she thought and proceeded to drive home.

Sirrah noticed Bennie mulling around at games and practice. He also worked as a bartender/waiter at the campus bar, the Rathskellar. The basketball team regularly converged on the Rathskellar after practices and games, especially if they won. Sometimes Sirrah went thereto relax after a hard day. Sirrah had her first taste of alcohol at the Rathskellar. Sirrah was well disciplined and never drank too much. Shenever did anything in excess, for that matter, and prided herself on being responsible. She ordered a Lemon Smash Cocktail. He spent the evening flattering her. Bennie told Sirrah that she was the most beautiful girl in the world as he mixed her cocktails. He never charged her for the drinks.

Bennie managed to appear wherever Sirrah was as if he knew her schedule. He called himself her number one fan. It was apparent that she intrigued him. He left flowers and gifts at her gym locker. He rooted for Sirrah, in particular, at games. If she sneezed, he showed up with a tissue. He waited for her after practice to walk her to her car no matter the weather. He went out of his way until he got her attention. She thought he was just another nice guy, but her teammates labeled him her stalker. That pissed Sirrah off and drew her closer to Bennie. She favored the underdog. She didn't tolerate teasing or bullying. Her teammates' teasing about him swayed her affection toward him. He gave Sirrah his undivided attention. He had a way of looking at her that made her feel like she was the only one on the planet.

Bennie went to Johnny B to ask about Sirrah's dating situation. Johnny B told him Sirrah was single and available but prefaced his statement by saying Sirrah would probably turn him down. Johnny B didn't know anything about Bennie thinking he was just another love-struck admirer of Goddess Sirrah. He was sure that Sirrah would shred Bennie's self-esteem if he approached her, the way she did other men who tried to get a date. Sirrah never had a boyfriend. She went on dates, but nothing serious ever came about. Sirrah was a virgin and proud of her purity, not that it was anyone's business. She wasn't dating and had no prospects when she met Bennie.

Bennie continued to observe Sirrah, waiting for his opportunity. He was ready to give up when he found out she was having difficulty with chemistry. Bennie told Sirrah that he was studying to get his Bachelors in Education. He excelled in mathematics and chemistry. Taking this opening, Bennie mustered up the courage to approach her. He offered to help Sirrah with her studies as a way to spend quality time with her. She initially declined. Sirrah already had a tutor and was busy with practice and studying. She couldn't put anything more on her plate. He said he was a chemistry major and offered to tutor her for free. The offer of free tutoring changed her mind. Although she paid a tutor, Sirrah found it difficult to coordinate their schedules. Bennie's volunteering to work himself into her schedule for free convinced her to drop the other tutor. They agreed to three sessions a week at the gym before basketball practice. This agreement worked perfectly for Sirrah. Since he was so accommodating and willing to help her, she offered to take him to lunch. He said yes, jumped up, and clicked his heels. Sirrah blushed at his enthusiasm. She thought he was a nerd with a crush.

During lunch, Sirrah was surprised and delighted to discover that he was smart, funny, and he adored her. Bennie was an excellent tutor. After three months of tutoring. Sirrah was beginning to like him, impressed by his intelligence, and entertained the prospect of a romantic relationship. She had no idea that Bennie studied her and already figured out how to get to her heart.

Bennie pretended to be interested in playing basketball and asked Sirrah to teach him how to play. He had ulterior motives to initiate physical contact. She thought playing against someone with Bennie's height would help to improve her game. She agreed with that in mind. Bennie was awkward, uncoordinated, and he couldn't dribble to save his life. She could run circles around him on the basketball court despite his trying hard. The fact that he tried to play was endearing. Their practice was short-lived. Sirrah refused to waste her time and told him to forget basketball and stick to tutoring. Bennie reluctantly admitted that he was not interested in basketball. He was interested in her. Sirrah responded, that's what you should have said in the first place, jokingly calling him a coward.

Sirrah developed a soft spot in her heart for Bennie. They had intellectually stimulating conversations. He demonstrated characteristics that reminded her of her father. They started to date. Bennie was a bartender at the Rathskellar, a tutor, and a part-time information technology specialist. He worked hard, and he was kind-hearted. He told Sirrah that he lived with four other students to share living expenses. He struggled to pay his tuition and room and board. Bennie never had money. He explained that the living conditions were not the best but better than what he had in his native home. Bennie didn't talk about his native country or his family as if he had a dark secret to hide. Sirrah never knew how many sisters and brothers he had.

As they grew to know each other, Sirrah learned not to pressure Bennie for information about his past. He would get irritated to the point of leaving or not communicating with her when she asked too many questions. Bennie would avoid her after their conflict, sometimes for days at a time. They could talk about anything except his past or family. He reluctantly spoke about his mother. She lived in the U.S., but he never said her actual location. They were almost three years into the relationship before Sirrah met her at a restaurant. Bennies mother's name is Makeba. After their initial meeting, Sirrah made sure to acknowledge his mother with cards and gifts on special days. Makeba never said thank you or accepted her. Sirrah did not take exception because she was in love with Bennie, not his mother. Sirrah assumed his situation was too traumatic for him to discuss. She suggested counseling, but he refused. She believed that she would find out everything in time.

Sirrah allowed him to leave his past a secret while confiding everything about herself, including her financial situation. She told him how she felt when her father died, and she felt the insurance money was blood money. Bennie never reacted to dating a rich girl. He said it was the man's duty to take care of the family. Every time he needed something, he would bring it up to Sirrah. Throughout their relationship, Bennie spent her money. He made indirect suggestions and requests for things that only benefited him. He acted frustrated or angry in front of Sirrah, knowing that she would try to find out what's wrong. Bennie let her extract information and offer her assistance. He gained access to her pockets by telling her his problems. She took that as a sign of trust and did whatever she could to help him. He discovered her weakness and took control of her life. Sirrah was a fixer. If Sirrah had what somebody needed, she would help—especially those she loved, and she had fallen in love with Bennie. She was in love with him before they had sex.

Sarah wanted to introduce Bennie to her family. He was resistant when she first mentioned it, saying he didn't have enough to present himself as a good dating prospect. He didn't even have a car. Sirrah had already mentioned him to her mother and would not take no for an answer. Bennie reluctantly agreed to meet her family. Johnny B was shocked when Sirrah brought him home. Johnny B had no idea that Sirrah was seeing Bennie. He forgot that Bennie inquired about her. Bennie showed up for dinner and finessed everyone except Zahara. Bennie was all smiles and well-spoken, saying things that should have comforted Zahara. She said something about him was "Not quite right." Sirrah's mother wasn't buying his attitude about not discussing his pastor his family. She told Sirrah point blank to be careful of people that don't talk about their life. They are usually hiding something. Zahara said until Bennie comes clean with whatever it is he's hiding, they should not move their relationship forward. Sirrah was disappointed. She would later find that her mother was right not to trust Bennie.

Sirrah complained to Bennie that her mother treated her like a child. That was all Bennie needed to hear to move his plan forward. She was devastated, and Bennie consoled her. Now he had a legitimate reason to steer clear of her family. Determined that she would not put Bennie in the position to be judged by her family again, with a little nudging from Bennie, Sirrah decided that she would lie to her mother about their relationship. Sirrah distanced herself from her family and secretly continued to date him. Her alone time with Bennie became limited when she no longer needed a tutor, but she always tried to make time for him. She spent whatever free time she had with him. Sirrah was happy to have a boyfriend. She did what she could to please him. Sirrah gave Bennie her virginity. As far as her family was concerned, Sirrah didn't have a boyfriend. Sirrah pretended to date others when there wasno one else but Bennie in her life. She was living a lie, and that was a big mistake.

Sirrah's schedule remained hectic, with basketball practice and school. She and Bennie would call or text to keep in contact when theywere not together. Bennie was free to do whatever he wanted while shewas away. He let Sirrah know that his mother was trying to set him up with women from their homeland. Makeba did not believe in monogamy, and that made it difficult for him not to go astray. Bennie upset Sirrah because she gave him her virginity to prove to him how much she loved him, and she belonged to him and only him. That still was not enough. Bennie said that moving in together would solve everything, plus they could use the money that he paid for rent to invest in their future. Sirrah had a difficult decision to make. Throwing her morals and upbringing out of the window, Sirrah gave in. She agreed that they would live together. After all, she wanted to spend her life with only him. Sirrah was happy at first, but thoughts of her mother and father nagged at her conscience. They told her never to shack up with aman outside of marriage because he wouldn't respect her in the long run. She clearly heard her dead father's voice saying, "He won't buy thecow if he can get the milk for free." Sirrah convinced herself otherwise,saying that was back in the day. Things are different now. Sirrah was also concerned that Bennie wanted her to secure a home for both of them. She knew that Bennie was having a hard time making ends meet, and she tried to help him over the hump. She thought he had a bright future once he graduated. Sirrah also enjoyed having Bennie to snuggle up with at night.

She thought things would get better if she moved into an apartment first and then move in Bennie later. They could live together, and no one would be the wiser. She intended to continue to deceive her family about their relationship until she graduated. She was so hungry for Bennie that she could lick him like he was a chocolate ice cream cone. Sirrah was foolishly in love. She rented an apartment for her and Bennie. She kept her mouth shut, even with Johnny B. It was the hardest thing she had ever done in her life. Her mother never found out she lived with Bennie; she never talked about it if she did. Zahara let Sirrah make decisions for herself. She definitely would have discussed it with Sirrah if she knew.

Sirrah managed to graduate summa cum laude with a bachelor of science in marketing and finance. She got a job with great benefits making $80,000. She worked and sacrificed to be the best, and it paid off. Bennie was right there in the midst of her celebration. Sirrah still had to figure out how to get her mother to accept Bennie. She was happy that the people she loved were celebrating her accomplishments together. She stopped playing league basketball shortly after she graduated. She was not interested in pursuing a professional career as a basketball player. The prospects of her becoming a pro athlete were slim. She would occasionally beat up on Johnny B on the court.

Bennie had problems landing a steady job, so he decided to freelance as an Informational Systems Specialist and taught a couple of online classes. He was agitated, saying that his degree was worthless. He felt education was the wrong field to choose. He could seem to find his passion. He had student loans and a car note, and insurance to pay. He was still struggling to make ends meet. By this time, Sirrah was paying all of their living expenses. Oddly enough, he started to pressure Sirrah about having a baby.

Chapter 4

Bennie popped the question on New Year's Eve. It as his effort to prove his worth and to solidify their relationship. He rented space on the Princess Riverboat and invited her family and closest friends, sparing no expense. He presented her with a two-karat, princess-cut diamond. That night he promised Sirrah the world in front of her family and friends. No one in his family was there.

Zahara was furious when her daughter accepted Bennie's proposal. She went to the upper deck of the ship to calm down. Sirrah noticed her mother's reaction and followed her. Zahara told her that Bennie was a parasite and washed her hands of the situation. Hugging Sirrah, she said, "It's your wagon. You can pull it or push it. If you marry poorly, you will be pushing for the rest of your life." Zahara wiped her tears away as they went back to the celebration together. Zahara went to Bennie and politely threatened Bennie saying, "Harm my baby, and I will hunt you down like the rabid dog that you are, and you know what happens to dogs." Then, she congratulated him. Zahara's eyes were shooting daggers as she walked away. Bennie appeared shaken. Sirrah rushed to his side to ask what her mother said. He knew Sirrah was worried about her mother's reaction, so he lied, saying Zahara said congratulations. That put Sirrah's heart at ease.

Bennie believed a big house was a status symbol. He decided they needed a larger home now that they were engaged. Sirrah bought a house in her name only because Bennie had credit problems. He did not contribute a dime towards the purchase. All Bennie did was help move both of them in. Bennie's refusal to discuss his family, his lousy credit, her family disapproval, and purchasing a home for them both didn't matter. She ignored her feelings because she loved her new house. Sirrah overlooked the red flags thinking that love would be enough for their relationship to survive.

The years passed quickly, with Bennie pressuring Sirrah to have achild before marriage. Sirrah would hold up her left hand's ring finger and say, "Put a wedding ring on it," when Bennie brought up having children. Sirrah reminded him that giving her an engagement ring meant nothing without the wedding. They argued whenever she tried to set a wedding date. Bennie made one excuse after another for putting the wedding off, saying he wasn't financially stable. He promised to choose a wedding date after he was secure in his job and paid off his debts. There was always a reason to put the wedding off. His to-do list increased over the years.

Despite his financial concerns, he still tried to bully Sirrah into having a child before marriage. He would argue that children represented abundance and wealth in his native country. According to his mother, Bennie was disgracing his family because his woman had not conceived a child. To be involved with a woman as long he was with Sirrah, Bennie should have a house filled with children. His mother called him impotent. Sirrah noticed that this was the only time he wanted to talk about his family. Sirrah let Bennie know that she doesn't care what his momma or anybody else in his family had to say. It goes against Sirrah's moral code to have a baby outside of marriage. She told him to go home and find someone else to pump full of big head babies. Bennie threatened to do just that. Bennie's attitude changed. He was rude and inconsiderate. She noticed that he stopped holding the door for her, and his hugs and kisses less frequent. The spark in his eyes had dimmed for Sirrah.

One time Bennie did leave after an argument. He was gone for two days. He left without taking any clothes or his phone. Sirrah was at her wits end. After twenty-four hours, Sirrah began to worry. She could not sleep or eat. She contacted the police and learned that you have to wait 48 hours to make a missing person report for an adult. Bennie came home with flowers before the 48-hour deadline. Sirrah was happy to see him that she forgot why she was mad. That marked the beginning of his control. Sirrah relinquished her power when she begged him never to leave her again. Bennie had full control of their relationship. Sirrah became compliant and passive to keep from arguing with him. He trained her not to question him.

The times that Sirrah spent with Bennie's mother were awkward. Makeba's attitude was nasty. She openly showed

Sirrah she was not pleased with her as a potential bride for her son through her facial expressions and standoffish mannerisms. The woman strutted around like a peacock, sucking her teeth whenever she looked at Sirrah. Makeba insulted Sirrah by calling her skin and bones, saying she needs to eat more. Makeba would not let Sirrah help her at all. She wouldn't accept anything, not even a glass of water, from Sirrah. Sirrah had never met aperson that didn't like her. This woman was arrogant as they come, always talking about the motherland. Sirrah tried to speak to Bennie about his mother, and he made excuses for Makeba's behavior. Saying she was overprotective and wouldn't like anyone for her Bennie. He assured Sirrah that it would get better once they got to know each other. Sirrah wanted to tell Makeba to take her fat butt home if this country isso horrible, but she respected her elder. Sirrah was sad that she could not discuss Makeba's behavior with her mother because she still didn't like Bennie, and Sirrah didn't want to make matters worse. Sirrah knew her momma would put Makeba and Bennie in their places for messing with her daughter. She didn't want her mother to tell her to put Bennie out. Sirrah was still not ready to give Bennie up.

In Bennie's mind, the baby issue prevented their relationship from being perfect. The fact that Sirrah wouldn't have his child was his major complaint. His logic didn't make sense to Sirrah, and she stood her ground. If Bennie was not stable enough to spring for a wedding, how the hell did he expect to take care of a child for eighteen years? It was bad enough that she allowed him to move in with her, and she also paidthe lion's share on the bills. The couple was turning out to be unequally yoked in every aspect of their relationship. Sirrah could compile a list of Bennies faults, and he still was not paying his way. She was still hopeful that things would get better.

Their relationship situation seemed to worsen over the years. Bennie would pick fights with her about the baby at least once a week. It had gotten so bad that Sirrah didn't enjoy being intimate anymore. He seemed to be on a mission to put a baby in her by plowing away at her intimately. He had become intense and aggressive sexually. She thought it was his moment of passion and climax in the beginning. She wondered if it was typical for sex to hurt. He was her only sexual partner. She had no other point of reference. If Sirrah brought it up, he got loud and verbally abusive. She learned to be quiet and take it.

Benny had become less of a love interest and more of a deadbeat roommate. Sirrah had become weary of the conflict and set a mental deadline of when she would be done with their relationship, giving him five more years to marry her. Sirrah stopped pressing Bennie about marriage and focused on her career after two years of waiting to set a date. She excelled in her craft out of frustration, putting the time she would have spent on wedding planning into work planning. She was promoted to Assistant Director of Finance for a major marketing firm,making six figures and wondering how much money is enough for marriage. The marriage deadline was winding down, and so was her biological clock. She didn't want to reach thirty without a wedding band on her finger and at least one child because she didn't want to waste her best years with Bennie.

Chapter 5

Sirrah was in her late twenties with no children and approaching the fifth year of her too-long engagement. Sirrah's mother did not like her daughter living with a man outside of marriage. Zahara made no secret about her feelings, saying, "If Nicholas were alive, you would not have moved a man into your house. Bennie couldn't buy a home for you. Your father would turn over in his grave if he knew you were living in sin and taking care of a man." Sirrah's father believed a man is not a man if he did not provide a home for his family. Sirrah was beginning to think her mother was right. Sirrah got another promotion to Finance Director. Her new position included a significant pay hike, a company vehicle with a chauffeur, an expense account, and yearly performance incentives. She worked her way to the top. Sirrah was feeling excited and proud of herself and rushed home to share the news with her fiancé. The only thing Bennie said was, "I guess you won't have time for a baby, for sure now." He asked her how she planned to fit having his child in with her new work responsibilities. She sarcastically responded she would work it out right after the wedding. Bennie went into a long tirade about American women not making good wives because of their ambition. Bennie's mother warned him against dating Sirrah. She ignored his comments. She was not going to let him rain on her parade. Every so often, she would respond to him with a sarcastic remark to hurt his feelings. She said, "You complain about American women, but you don't complain about using their American money."

Sirrah called her mother and her friends to share the news about her promotion. They agreed to celebrate. Bennie continued to harangue her with his issues with American women's ambition as she dressed. She showered, selected a sexy black mini dress, and adorned her feet with silver and black Giuseppe Zanotti stilettos. Sirrah dressed, thinking that Benny would take one look at how beautiful and sexy his fiancé was and forget all about arguing. Instead, she heard the door slam in the background. She yelled, "Bye, Felicia," loud enough for him to hear onthe way out. Bennie was gone. He had a habit of abruptly leaving the house and staying away for days when Sirrah made him angry. This time seemed no different.

Bennies' reaction to her promotion made Sirrah think he might be jealous. Money was not an issue for Sirrah, while Bennie barely made ends meet. Bennie didn't have to be rich. Sirrah only wanted a faithful, loving husband who contributed financially to the household. He didn't realize that if she made more money, they could do whatever they wanted, including getting married. Sirrah couldn't believe he was mad and treated her like she did something wrong. She grabbed her white Dolce and Gabbana trench coat and left without giving him another thought. Her girls were waiting for her. They were happy to celebrate her success, even if Bennie wasn't. "Bennie could go jump in a lake and drown." she thought.

Sirrah partied and danced until her feet were sore. She forgot about her troubles. Drinks were flowing at the club, and the men were exceptionally nice to Sirrah. She had a blast. Feeling happy that she made it home safely, she went straight to bed without showering. She had too much to drink. She barely got her clothes off. It was after three in the morning when she got home, and Bennie was not there.

***

The sunlight blazing through the Venetian blinds woke her up at ten o'clock. She checked her phone, and there was no word from Bennie. Thinking he was probably on one of his stays at his momma's house, she rolled over and went back to sleep. It was around noon before she woke up again and mustered enough energy to shower. The warm water cascading over her naked silhouette helped her relax. She peeped through the shower curtain and noticed that Bennie's toothbrush and shaving kit were gone from the bathroom vanity. She thought that was strange as he usually left those when he went to his momma's. She reached for a towel and found none. Sirrah muttered aloud, "What the hell?" as she pushed open the shower door and stepped onto the cold ceramic tile floor. The bathroom rug was gone. Sirrah grabbed her robe, noticing that Bennie's robe was not on the hook next to hers. She ran to the bedroom. At first glance, everything seemed normal until she opened the door to his wardrobe closet. Bennie's clothes were gone, and his chest of drawers was empty. It looked like the piece of shit moved out. It was too early, and she had too many lemon slushies in her system from the night before. She did not want to deal with Bennie's crap. She brewed coffee to sober up and went to sit on the balcony. She fully intended to enjoy her alone time. She was not going to chase Bennie. He was not worth the grief. She chuckled, thinking this might be a good thing.

Saturday passed into Sunday morning with no word from Bennie. Readying herself for church service, Sirrah went to her shoe closet for the first time since Bennie left. Without looking, she reached for her black Christian Louboutin pumps and felt nothing. Her shoes were missing. A knot swelled in her stomach as she glanced across the shelves where the rest of her shoes (or "babies," as she affectionately called them) lived. She let out a bloodcurdling scream. "He took my shoes!"

Her heart pounded as she ran to her wardrobe closet, and it was empty. She rushed her chest of drawers. As she pulled them open one by one and each drawer was empty. Bennie took her lingerie. She could not believe her eyes. Sirrah panicked as she approached the nightstand, where she kept her jewelry. With trembling hands, she pulled the bronze knob of the upper drawer. She held her breath as the drawer opened, revealing nothing. Bam! Her body hit the floor with a thud. Sirrah passed out.

Sirrah woke up with a splitting headache. She was still on the floor. She lay there for what seemed to be an eternity, processing what just happened. How could Bennie do this to her? She crawled to the bed, struggling with a fierce headache. She reached for the house phone to dial his number. Sirrah dialed Bennie's number and heard a recorded message saying the phone was outside of the provider's range.

Sirrah called Makeba to question her about Bennie, but before she could say anything, his mother said they were in Canada preparing to board a flight to Africa. Bennie acquired enough money to live wealthy, and they were going home. Sirrah told her that Bennie stole her money. Makeba called Sirrah a silly American and said, "I will pray for you to make better choices in the future with your next boyfriend. You must learn from this mistake. I hope you find someone to make you happy. " Sirrah called her a ruthless witch. She heard Bennie laughing in the background. She went numb as the phone disconnected. Sitting on the bed paralyzed, Sirrah forced herself to breathe. Her thoughts and emotions bounced from one extreme to another. She was angry, embarrassed, and hurt all at once. She felt too stupid to cry. Sirrah felt like a zombie.

Chapter 6

The day was gone. Sirrah lost track of time. She didn't go to church. The cold night air from the open balcony brought Sirrah back to the present. She had been sitting in the same spot for hours, trying to figure out what she was going to do. Not only did Benny leave her, but he robbed her. Sirrah reasoned Bennie broke a glass pane in the side door during a previous argument, and that validated making a burglary claim on her homeowners' insurance. She called the police to make a report. It was the only way she would be able to recoup some of her material losses. This situation made Sirrah wonder who was the man that she slept with every night? Sirrah felt like the dumbest woman on earth. As she attempted to figure out how this could happen to her, she reflected on how they met. She had an epiphany. Sirrah rationalized that their relationship was no more than a diabolical scheme to take her money.

Bennie deliberately removed all traces of himself from their house. There were no pictures. He refused to allow her to post images of him on social media, spouting some bull crap that using his image would cast a curse on his soul and take his spirit. She had one photo of him in the background of an event when she inadvertently caught him in a panoramic shot. No utilities were under his name, not even his phone, which was in Sirrah's.

Their relationship didn't start that way. Bennie always presented a valid reason for having all their utilities in Sirrah's name temporarily. He processed himself out of her life over the years. He even sent his mail to a post office box because it was close to his job. How convenient was that? He was able to disassociate his name from her address.

Sirrah discovered that Bennie also used her identity to establish credit lines and opened accounts in her name, making online purchases of big-ticket items. Bennie also maxed out her credit cards and used her ATM cards. Fearing Bennie might have sold her information Sirrah locked all of her accounts and indicated that she is notified of all transactions. Bennie stole about $100,000. He changed her passwords and email address so she couldn't access her accounts. Sirrah had no idea of when he changed her information. She trusted him with everything.

Sirrah had unanswered questions and needed to know more. Still trying to maintain privacy, she didn't want to hire a private investigator. She did it herself. Sirrah went to the place Bennie lived before he latched onto her. She uploaded an address that she found on one of his old envelopes, and it was a storefront that provided mailbox addresses instead of P.O. boxes. Stunned at what she saw, Sirrah sat in her car in disbelief. There was no reason to go in. She had never been to his house. He talked about living in deplorable conditions that made her never want to visit. His story of living with five guys was false. She felt like this was some elaborate prank or a bad dream. She was going to wake up, and her life would be normal again.

Sirrah remembered that Bennie had friends who owned a clothingstore on Livernois Avenue, at the Avenue of Fashion. She and Bennie occasionally had dinner with them. Sirrah purchased several outfits from the store to support their business. Bennie gave her the impression that he grew up with these people. Thinking they might know where Bennie was, she decided to visit them. Sirrah arrived at the shop during lunch hour. She stood outside, contemplating what to say without revealing what Bennie did. She didn't want them to tip Bennie off just in case he was still in Detroit. When Sirrah finally mustered up enough courage and entered the shop, Evie, the owner, stopped working and came to greet her. She embraced Sirrah, looking around as if expecting Bennie to be with her. Evie asked, "What can I do for you, darling?" All the things Sirrah intended to say went out of her mind.

Sirrah bluntly said, "I'm looking for Bennie. He took everything I owned and left. Do you know where he is?" Evie was genuinely caught off guard by what Sirrah said. Evie explained, "Bennie and his wife came in about a week ago to settle an outstanding tab because they were leaving the country." Sirrah's mouth dropped as she repeated, "Wife?" She asked, "Was Bennie already married?" Sirrah's reaction made Evie stop talking. Evie took a good look to notice the color drained from Sirrah's face. She was pale as a ghost. Evie guided Sirrah to an office in the back of the store, where they could talk privately.

Evie told Sirrah they didn't know Bennie from Africa. The first time Evie met Bennie, he came into the store with Makeba. Makeba was a heavyset older woman. Initially, Evie thought the woman was his mother because he called her mommy. Evie found it strange that Bennie acted familiar with his mother. She witnessed them hold hands, and Bennie would touch her in ways that a man would caress a wife. He would pat her on the bottom and hug her in a manner that was not appropriate for a mother. It was later that Makeba told Evie she was Bennie's wife. Bennie said Sirrah was a wealthy woman philanthropist who was like family. She helped them when they came to the states. Bennie's wife, Makeba, came in more frequently to make purchases.

Sirrah explained that Bennie was her fiancé, and they lived together. Evie let Sirrah know that they were not a part of Bennie's shenanigans. They didn't believe in a man having more than one wife. Sirrah was shocked to learn that the woman she thought was Bennie's mother was his wife. Sirrah purchased gifts and broke bread with this woman. His wife/mother, Makeba, was a tragic waste of womanhood for participating in the ruse.

Sirrah realized the man that she planned to marry was a stranger. The fact that she gave the gift of her virginity to Bennie felt like a dagger in her heart. She violated her promise to God to remain celibate. Sirrah felt sick to her stomach at the thought of being deceived. Evie genuinely attempted to console Sirrah by saying she was sorry that Bennie robbed her. She had no idea that he was that type of low life. If they knew what Bennie was up to, her husband would have beaten him in the dirt. Evie assured Sirrah that they would spread the word in their community about what Bennie did. They would do everything in their power to help find him, but he was probably long gone. Evie said she didn't want any trouble because of Bennie. Sirrah gave Evie her phone number and left. Once again, Sirrah sat in her car, wondering how she let this happen to her. In hindsight, a lot of pieces began to fit together. Her family's intuition about Bennie was right; they hated him. She could never tell her mother the truth.

Sirrah ruminated on events during their relationship that she now saw in a different light: She gave Bennie money and let him use her car to go on vacation with his "wife." She thought of the times that she got out of her warm bed to pick up Makeba from the airport and the numerous times she purchased clothes, birthday gifts, and Christmas presents for the woman. The fact that Sirrah fed, clothed, and slept with Bennie wasn't bad enough. The thought of him sleeping with both her and Makeba in her house challenged Sirrah's mental stability. Sirrah felt like she wanted to die.

From then on, Sirrah functioned on auto-pilot, going through the motions of living. She watched from the sidelines as her life passed by like a black-and-white film. Her taste buds were dead, and her appetite was nonexistent. Food tasted like warmed-over cardboard. She lost twenty pounds in a month. People complimented her on how good she looked on the outside, not knowing inside she was no longer alive. She was a walking zombie, moving about, void of emotional connection. She had crying spells and wanted to kill something all at the same time. One thing she did not feel was happiness, and she struggled to fake it. She was losing her mind.

Recovery from the material loss was easy. The emotional damage was devastating. How would Sirrah get over the emotional carnage left by Bennie? Still wanting to avoid embarrassment, Sirrah told no one other than Evie of Bennies' treacherous deed and her vulnerable state. If anyone found out the truth, the humiliation would kill her. She made up another reason for their break up.

Zahara tried to console Sirrah with prayer and hugs. She told Sirrah that it was for the best that they took so long to marry. Not knowing the whole story, she said Bennie would have cleaned her out if they were married. Sirrah cringed hearing that. She couldn't tell her mother that he already did. It did not feel right to conceal the truth from her mother. Only God knew the truth, and Sirrah couldn't even pray.

Sirrah wanted to stop the pain, so she decided to kill herself. She thought her mother, grandmother, Johnny B, and the rest of her family and her friends would be devastated by the loss of her. The only one in her universe who didn't love her was the predator, Bennie. Though she realized killing herself would hurt everyone except the one who deserved it, but the thought stayed on her mind. She couldn't feel the presence of God anywhere. She wanted so badly to feel faith like her mother, but she only felt sorrow. She needed her mother and longed for her strength and confidence. Sirrah contemplated how to end it all. She prayed that God would allow her to die.

It occurred to Sirrah to write a note expressing her torment and leave a record of what she was feeling inside because she appeared normal on the outside. Her fake life was all smiles and happiness. No one knew how badly she wanted to die. She wanted her family to know that her death was not their fault.

Taking pen in hand, Sirrah had a tantrum on paper. She let the angry, bitter bitch that Bennie created have her way, but only on paper. For months she penned her innermost feelings. Her thoughts were dark and focused on her trauma. She wrote anything she was feeling and everything she wanted to say. Her thoughts evolved from hate to love as she devised her exit plan. No matter how badly she wanted to die, God said not so. The suicide notes began to liberate her emotionally. She never got around to an actual suicide attempt.

Sirrah's Notes

A broken heart is a fickle thing. A brokenhearted person experiences a gambit of emotions. They are ups and downs, anger and despair, love, and hate. Sometimes all at the same time. One feeling hits you in the gut, and other emotions hit you in the head. Sirrah's Notes are 86 reflections of her transformation from a wounded and brokenhearted woman to one with spiritual and mental liberation.

Note 1

Nobody knows how I feel. My insides are torn and shattered like broken glass. Rage builds inside of me that I fear will never pass. Dying seems like the only way out. I only have God to hold on to, and my grip is not that strong. I will meet him soon. I have plans to leave this body,but I have one concern that bounds me to this earth. I hope God will explain away this misery. It would be a shame to die and still have these feelings in the spirit. The only thing that keeps me here is fear.

Note 2

Bennie, I write to satisfy the part of me that wants to pick up a brick to throw through your mother's window because she birthed you. I write to satisfy the urge to find you and slap the taste out of your mouth. I write to keep from whipping you like you stole something, which your momma should have done during your formative years. I write so that I can maintain a peaceful countenance as I go about my day. I pen the rage within me with hopes it will subside before I do something criminal.

Note 3

Today my thoughts moved from suicide to homicide. I had thoughts of killing everyone associated with your existence. I figured out how I would do it and was on my way. I got distracted because I couldn't find my car keys. I spent the entire day looking for them. It's a thin line between sane and insane. Thank God!

Note 4

I loved you more. Bennie, you loved me never. I looked for your face in every crowd. I am never giving up on the prospect of finding you. You are always on my mind. I look for you amidst the sun, the earth, and the moon. I have clarity, peace, and serenity now that I know for sure you are gone. I pray that your spirit is resting in heaven. If I allow myself to think of you alive, I would be forced to hunt you down and kill you where you stand.

Note 5

He killed me before my body knew it was dead.

He ripped my heart from my chest before I could react.

He put it in a blender with the setting on puree.

He prepared it like a bloody mary cocktail and drank it.

He left bitterness where my heart once resided.

Note 6

My mind finally comprehended what my heart didn't want to believe. You didn't love me. You didn't want me. You used me for my money. You pursued me, even slept with me. What manner of a man are you? You are a devil with no soul seeking to steal, kill, and destroy. I had no way of knowing the outcome of our encounter, but you did. I think you knew from the start what you were going to do. What you wanted was my happiness. I couldn't believe how far you were willing to go to take it.

Note 7

You should be arrested for being so fine with your six-pack and buns of steel. Bennie, your billy club exceeds eight inches. Yeah! You should be arrested for false advertising.

Note 8

The world won't allow *love* to reign. The world mocks love, pointing its finger. The world laughs behind love's back. The world questions love's value. The world partners with *lack* to destroy love. The world makes men fight over love. The world makes women cry over love. The world makes love cry at heaven's gate. The world pushes love out, making more room for hate.

Note 9

She lives inside of the heart of me. She is the me that nobody knows. Her wrath is ferocious. Her vengeance is complete. The fire in her is all-consuming. She is waiting to burst out of my soul. She lurks behind my smiling face waiting to reclaim what you stole.

Note 10

My emotions are raw because of this reckless encounter. Fear holds me hostage. Now I am afraid to shine. God has given me a brilliant, analytical mind. I hide behind a superficial, biological façade; I was pretending to be less than I am. I feared my shine would cause you to go blind.

Note 11

There were always reasons why you were right, and everyone else was wrong. Your give-me-what-I-want-or-hit-the-road-Jack attitude was not a recipe for success. Bennie, you are a parasite. You stick to your host, extracting money, love, and life from those who encounter you. Even your mother was a victim of giving you life.

Note 12

Why am I blue? Because of you!

Note 13

Bennie, you are the one that horror movies warn about. Jason Voorhees and Freddy Krueger would be scared of you. You would devour the resources of Jason and wear his mask as a trophy on your belt. You would put poor Freddy to work harvesting females for you, gutting them like catfish and making filets. I fear for anyone that falls prey to you. You win.

You are the best at what you do. You are the ultimate monster!

Note 14

I gave you the best of me, Bennie. You scowled and frowned and asked for the rest. I have nothing left but the shadow of my former self. I know why Cain slew Abel. If God's rejection made him feel as I do right now. It's a deep-rooted hurt that comes from a damaged soul. It's a bitterness gone out of control. It's hard to be in pain, and the one that is hurting you proceeds as if you don't exist. They are unreachable, untouchable, and unlovable. I ask God for forgiveness for my evil, wicked, sinful ways, for putting a man before him. I want this man to know how badly I hurt. He will never allow me the opportunity. He already knows. He just doesn't care.

Note 15

You kissed me and killed me at the same time. Bennie, you took part of my essence each time we kissed. You breathed and absorbed my soul each time you inhaled. You depleted me with each caress. You soaked in my beauty. With each glance, I became less and less attractive to myself. To continue with you, I will surely lose myself. To stay with you, I would die.

Note 16

I loved freely, if only for a moment. Love cannot exist in the environment of hate. Hate replaces love when there is malice. Fear replaces love when there is a danger. Anger replaces love when there is pain. Love is blamed for damage other emotions caused. Love can be beautiful if it is left alone.

Note 17

I said goodbye to love today. Not only does love not love me, it tried to murder me. It sucked the joy and laughter out of me. It choked and squished the blood out of my heart. It almost took my life. Love gutted me like a fish. It left me lying in a pool of blood. I appeared lifeless. I heard *love* laugh as it walked away, taking for granted that I was deceased. Now, I struggle to live without it. I make sure to avoid love for fear that it might return to finish the job.

Note 18

My heart is broken into pieces. It leaks blood with every beat. I need to heal, but I don't know how to. I finally see you for the con artist that you are, Bennie. You and I are both in love with you. We are unequally yoked. Your two hearts to leave me none. Zero only equals love in a tennis match.

Note 19

What did I lose when I lost you, Bennie?

- I lost arguing every day.

- I lost you begging for my money.

- I lost doing you favors that I don't want to do.

- I lost you not being affectionate.

- I lost you complaining about what you don't have.

- I lost your disrespect of me.

- I lost you treating me like I am your ATM.

- I lost nothing good. Losing you is a bonus for

me. I don't envy your next victim.

Note 20

Will I ever be whole again? You broke me down to a fraction of myself. My numerator is hurt, and my denominator pain. I declare myself a disaster area. I will keep dumping love into my half cup. I hope someone will come to fill it up. I will live, laugh, and love enough to turn my half a whole.

Note 21

Some call him a mack. Some call him a pimp. I call him treacherous. He victimizes innocent, unsuspecting females. He leeches off of women. He is called by various names. What I will not call him is a man!

Note 22

You tore through my life with a vengeance, Bennie. Like Hurricane Katrina with gale-force winds, you disrupted my soul and broke my heart. You came and went fast, leaving carnage and debris all around. My life was a disaster area, with no FEMA or other federal aid available to help me pick up the pieces. My only solace is the hope that someday someone will enter your life with the same destructive temperament. I hope they wreak havoc on your existence and tear you apart limb from limb until you cease to exist. Then and only then will the balance be restored in my universe. Vengeance will be mine!

Notes 23

Bennie was on a mission to seek and destroy. He pursued me, singing songs of love, catching me in all the right places. I was a bystander, but not innocent by a long shot. I willingly ignored the danger signs. I hoped something I did would change his mind. I wanted to feel wanted, and I wanted to be needed. His passion was my attraction. Did I infiltrate his world? Or did Bennie infiltrate mine? Does he love women or hate us with a passion? He didn't move from his position, but I played as if he did. He checked when I wanted to mate.

Note 24

He doesn't know my dreams. He doesn't see me. He looks through me like I am invisible. His real Love interest has his undivided attention. Her beauty blocks my image. She is the new car that he can hardly afford to drive. Hopefully, he will run out of gas. Maybe high gas prices will stop him from driving, and he will stop moving long enough to see me. Maybe!

Note 25

Man

If he sleeps with you, that doesn't mean he loves you. As a matterof fact, sex is merely an exercise. He can play ball, lift weights, or intercourse the most accessible cavern. A woman is just a warm hole.

Woman

If she sleeps with you, she is in love or aspiring to be loved. She wants a lifetime commitment but settles for right now. She is eager to please, competing with every other woman age eighteen and up. After the act, she rinses the waste from her receptacle with summer's eve.

She dreams of love everlasting while he dreams of getting a high score in his video game.

Note 26

Bennie, when I met you, and my heart missed a beat. I couldn't breathe as you crooned, "Do Me, Baby" and "Reasons." It was my delight to watch you perform. You made me feel special. Your representative was the man I met that day. He was the man of my dreams, but you sent him away. I had no idea you'd cause winter in mylife. I wanted your heart to be your wife. The dog that surfaced was insensitive and crass. If it were legal, I would beat your A$$.

Note 27

Like a dog, Bennie ate me up, regurgitated me, and left me for other dogs to finish. I vow to become sour and bitter. The next dog that eats me up will get sick and die.

Note 28

How do I love thee? Let me count the ways: One.

Damn, I guess I don't love you at all.

Note 29

When a man smiles at you, what does he mean?

Is he happy to see you?

Is he thinking of someone else, and you just happened to pass by?

Does he know that you needed a smile or you had a hard day?

Does he think this is another mark, someone to use and

abuse?

Is he smiling to lure you into a false sense of security?

Did he just get his false teeth whitened and want to show off thesparkle of his pearly white teeth?

Women never really know!

Note 30

I am not dead yet. I may be down, but don't count me out. My heart is critically wounded, but it still beats. I still have movement in my legs and feet. I will dance this dance of life, and only I will choreograph the next steps. No one else will control my rhythm this time. My dignity and self-respect are what I'm trying to find. I'll spin and twirl in the mirror to see if I can find the love and beauty that's me.

Note 31

It took losing you, Bennie, to find me. I lost myself in the enormous shadow that you cast over my life. I forgot that I am beautiful. I forgot about my curvy hips and my pretty eyes. A stranger complimented me, saying things you use to say and familiarly touched my hand. I was surprised. He said he remembered me from a past life. He said one day, I will become his wife. Then, I woke up.

Note 32

I call Bennie's name in the night only to hear my voice echo back to me. It bounces from wall to wall, then falls from the air because he's never there. I am a good woman; however, not flawless. His absence is a down, and his presence is an up. Maybe I have it twisted. When we are together, Bennie is critical, cynical, and unloving. When he is gone, I imagine the kind and loving gentleman he was when we first met. It becomes a problem when the downs are frequent, and the ups are few. Maybe the love I long for only exists in an alternate universe.

Note 33

If I must grow old alone, I'll choose to be happy with myself.

Note 34

At first, you were kind and a gentleman. You turned out to be ruthless and hardhearted. It didn't matter what you turned out to be. It was what I was when I was with you. I loved you without conditions. I was nothing to you, but I am valuable to me.

Note 35

In hindsight, I feel blessed to have experienced you. You helped me live outside of myself and to love despite the pain of loving you. I ignored the signs that you were untrue. You pushed me to love beyond loves limits. Because of you, I mastered agape. Because of you, I am Love. Thank you Bennie.

Note 36

Love is hurting me today. It's growing big inside me like an unborn child. It's developing within me, with no way out. It's getting too large for a natural delivery. My need to push and deliver love is way overdue. Somebody, anybody, please deliver it. I need a C-section for love.

Note 37

Unfortunately, our paths crossed in the night. Our bodies collided with intense delight. Blinded by the glitz and shine of your star, I dimmed my light to see who you are. Now I am lost in your shadow.

Note 38

Hurt is a vicious cycle. You hurt me, and I didn't get to hurt you back. I'll probably hurt someone else because of you. The someone I hurt will probably, hurt someone else because of me. I hurt, they hurt, we all harm other people in retaliation for past hurts. We spew wrath onto other people because they happened to get in the way. Victims will get caught in the crossfire. Hurt is vicious, and it doesn't mind crippling the innocent.

Note 39

A heart in turmoil eventually destroys the body, the mind, and thesoul. Life can leave a hole in your heart from the loss of someone you love. You cannot recuperate by withholding or abstain from life and living. Abstaining from love creates distress that eats at your soul like cancer.

Note 40

Music was our foreplay. Earth, Wind, and Fire gave us *reasons* to touch, kiss, and hold each other tight. These reasons couldn't sustain usin the morning light. You went your way, and I went mine. I blame myself for ignoring the hazard signs. The flash of your light blinded me. You fled from me like a hit-and-run accident. It's called no-fault in insurance terms.

Note 41

Love left me alone and insecure. It gave me pain that was hard to endure. Wanting and needing you. Bennie, you damaged me to my core. I sit beside myself, wiping my tears. I gave you my life and six of my years. I ask God to help to get over your pain. I wanted to hurt you, but that was insane.

Note 42

My most precious gift, I gave to you; and you threw it away. I cry and mourn for your love every day. I grow stronger, knowing that I still have the propensity to give my all. If I can share everything to an unworthy scumbag, I know now that I can be *every* woman, as Chaka Khan sang, to a real man.

Note 43

Is there another agenda at play? I still have the propensity and capabilities to love, but why did I choose you. You trivialized my needs. Our relationship was always about you. Your neglect tormented me. I pray that I can survive the residue of loving you.

Note 44

I've been looking for love for so long. I fear I won't recognize it if it stares me in the face. Thoughts of you blind me. You are always on my mind. I want to kiss away your tears and console you after a hard day. I love you with all my being. My heart and soul aches for you. I long to speak to you, it's me on the telephone line. I see you glaring at me with distaste and mistrust. I recoil at the sound of sarcasm in your voice when you interrogate me about having your child. You don't possess the qualities I want in a man. Yet I still long to hold and kiss you.

Note 45

Bad credit, liar, cheater, rude, inconsiderate were all on his resume. He gave me nothing. I went low to accommodate him only to realize that a loser rejected me. *Wow!*

Note 46

In a dream, I was a villain. I had a chance to go back to the point where I hurt a loved one, and I was allowed to fix it. The dream showed me that the adjustment points that I came to did not coincide with my victims' point of pain. I was allowed to experience their version of what happened, and I felt their pain first hand. Their pain was excruciating and intense. I will never again assume I know how another person feels. Our perception is not the reality of the one we hurt. I am glad it was just a dream.

Note 47

I am beside myself with grief. I suffer knowing that I was a fool for a low life like you. I pray for relief, hoping God will release me from the burden and embarrassment of loving you.

Note 48

WTF (Whiskey tango foxtrot) did I think when I gave you my love and affection, Bennie?

(Whiskey tango foxtrot) did you do that makes me want you so badly?

(Whiskey tango foxtrot) makes me long for you morning, noon, and night?

WTF is wrong with me?

Note 49

I think I hate you or do I hate me. How much I value myself is brought into question. I have to relearn how to love myself. I call back the parts of me from all unworthy men. I am challenging myself to move forward in my life. Each day I will take steps moving toward the goal of reincarnating myself. I look forward to who I will become.

Note 50

Why does love leave me every time? It doesn't matter what I do. If I turn to the right, love makes a left. If I go up, love takes a high swan dive or a low crawl into the caverns of the earth. Love avoided me all my life. I tried to be a good woman, even acted like a wife. I ache for the warm embrace of love. At least I think the embrace is warm. I'm guessing because I never felt it. When love comes knocking, I'm either in the bathroom or fast asleep. It's like my love is topsy-turvy, and I'm switching and missing letters or reading it backward. Love doesn't give a *this* about me.

Note 51

Bennie volleyed the love ball into my court. Then he quit playing the game before I could return the serve.

Note 52

The predicament in which I find myself is like a double-edged sword. One side is your wife, and me on the other. I see you smile the same smile at both of us. I see her look at you lovingly. It made me feel sad, angry, and hurt all at once. My heart raced fast, almost beating itself out of my chest. How did I get here? You are not my man or hers, for that matter. Both of us are victims of your selfishness.

Note 53

Bennie, I thought about you this morning. You were also in my thoughts throughout the day. I think about you when my phone doesn't ring. Your silence is screaming so loud. I wish I couldn't hear what you didn't say. My love didn't mean a thing.

Note 54

When I contemplate my life, it seems to be a comedy of errors. I live hard and play even harder. I have a lot of perishable toys. They usually break the day after the warranty expires, malfunctioning beyond repair, costing me the expense of pay full price for a new one. Maybe next time, I'll play it smart and discard the toy before the warranty expires. My perishable toys are men.

Note 55

I'm in a battle. I must fight to get my heart back from the men who destroyed it with broken promises of love and happiness. Failed relationships chipped away at my heart and devoured it bit by bit, piece by piece. I command the pieces of my heart to come forth as Lazarus. Come forth, live again in me.

Note 56

During our frequent fights, you'd say that you were leaving me, and my heart always froze. I trembled in silence, waiting for the punchline, but none came. I knew for sure you would leave me. It's the when, where, and how that burdened me to my core. I pondered what I would do when there is no more you?

Now that you are gone, I just go through the mechanics of living. How do I exist without the heart that I gave to you? There is a hole where my heart used to be. I couldn't believe that you didn't love me. Maybe I'll fill the empty space with skittles and call it a rainbow.

Note 57

What's the worst that can happen if he doesn't call?

Will I forget to breathe?

Will my heart turn cold, lose all feeling?

Will I become bitter?

Will I seek revenge on the next innocent man?

Will I continue to sit by the phone and wait?

I question my integrity. Have I hurt someone unknowingly?

Do I deserve to be punished?

All my self-preservation instincts ceased leaving me vulnerable.

I loved him more than I love myself. I need professional help,

and that's OK. This is not healthy. I'll make an appointment

today.

Note 58

I executed the former me. The loud mouthed witch me, with

the attitude. The me that wouldn't have taken this from a man.

The me that kept me from being hurt. She is posed in the

background of the pitiful me, waiting to *ooh* jack him up. I see

her right under the surface of the me that I present, the public

me. She is ready to strike. She is the epitomeof the angry Black

woman. I cannot control her or keep her calm. She remains

silent out of respect. She knows what I'm trying to do. She

permits me to act as our representative. She wants what I want

to be loved, honored, and cherished. She will stay subdued until

I say go. To unleash her wrath is to self-destruct.

Note 59

When I needed a man, you were never there, Bennie. I became

theaccessory you used for an appropriate occasion. After using

me, you castme into the bin with other discarded accessories.

There each accessory waits for the next occasion to be pinned to your chest. Maybe my turn will be next spring. My colors are pretty. I am red, black, and green. How will I sustain my beauty until then?

Wait! I think another accessory-seeker is coming. Maybe I can adorn his chest until my next outing with you. Until then, I will continue to shine for myself.

Note 60

I am a producer of life. I am the future, the mother, the wife. I am the result of God's ultimate sacrifice. I am *love*! Grab hold. Hold me close to your heart. Never let me go.

Note 61

Today I went to the river. When I got there, the weather was warm. As I bask in the sun, clouds began to accumulate, overcasting the sky. The breeze became almost cold, to the point of freezing, like our relationship. As I prepared to leave, the sun came up again and caressed my back with its warm embrace. Do I stay and wait for the ensuing storm? The wind is picking up, and I'm still here. Other people run for shelter, but I remain. I can weather the storm.
I can stand the rain if you let me. Can you, Bennie?

Note 62

I watched a young man catch a fish today. I watched him smile as it flipped and flopped on his hook. It was out of its element and unableto breathe. It was a beautiful bass, silver with streaks of blue. I watched as he held it in his hand and jerked the hook. I watched him as he watched the fish as it bled. Streams of blood ran down its beauty covering it with bright red. I watched him watch the fish as it died. Then, I watched him catch another fish. I liken the scenario to loving you, Bennie. Women are fish to you.

Note 63

Not a day goes by that I don't think of you, Bennie; wanting to touch and hold you, wanting to kiss your lips until our passion subsides. The pains of life cover your heart like a giant shield. I can't get in. I exhaust myself trying to chip away the pieces of your armor. I thought I cracked it once. You smiled and relaxed in my arms. That was a long time ago. Then another unfortunate circumstance gave your armor a makeover, soldering it together, resealing your heart into its tomb once again.

Note 64

Oh, Bennie! You presented yourself as a man from above. You sang to me, "Do Me, Baby" and "This Woman's Work." You lured mein with songs of love. Your beautiful voice was like a siren of old, attracting unsuspecting women, leading them to their inevitable destruction. The carcasses of females that you destroyed lay everywhere. You promised me you would always be there. Cherishing you was a mistake. I had no idea your love was fake.

Note 65

I gave my love to you one day. You took it, and you walked away. I was drunk with passion and caught in your whirlwind, Bennie. My heart was spinning and spinning. I was too drunk to get my bearings. You tossed me to and fro like a leaf in the wind. Then, I landed. Weak and frail, I didn't recognize myself as I crawled, searching to find fertile soil. Alas! No one told me that I landed in the desert where only Joshua trees and cactus thrive. With no place to anchor, there I died.

Note 66

I am every woman who's been wronged.

I am the child men that sired and left behind, without a father. I am the little girl that watched while her father degraded her mother. I am the teenager that a relative fondled while calling it tickling. I am thewoman raped, mistreated, and abused. I am the woman who can't trust enough to have a relationship. I am the wife who tolerates lying and cheating. I am the woman who left gave up material wealth to save her children and herself. I am the overcomer, the independent woman. I am the epitome of love. Stand back, and watch me grow. The pain is the same no matter the situation.

I am every woman.

Note 67

She wakes in the night alone. She cries, but no one hears. Her tears fall, leaving dry white streams to cover her face. No one sees her suffering. The tragedy of an undone woman was bestowed on her from birth. No one will ever know her pain. It is for only God to witness. She believes that womanhood is a virtue. She hides the holy grail from all seekers. She is patiently awaiting her tribute. She understands that she will probably have to go to heaven to hear it. Being a woman is a *blessing* and a *curse*.

Note 68

Love leaned on me hard one day. Love brought me through your trials and pain. Love said when it's over, I will remain. Love brought happiness, joy, and the fulfillment of my dreams. Love made me whole, so it seems. I remember love. The day you left, Bennie. It still lives within me. So proud of itself. Love wrapped its arms around me and said, don't cry? Love introduced me to loneliness when you said goodbye. Love said there is much that I must learn. Love did not wait for your return. God will give me a man who is faithful and true. He will provide me with the love that I never knew. I pray God heals your heart one day. Meanwhile, my new love is on the way.

Note 69

I dream of waking every morning with you by my side. I dream of walks on the beach, keeping pace with your stride. Sharing our hopes and conquering our fears, and being with you for the rest of my years was my goal. I loved you deeper than you could ever see, but our love could never be. You will always be you, and I will be me. Now I understand there was never *we*. I still have my hopes. Now I have my tears. Holding tight to a dream for the rest of my years, I will travel through life alone, so it seems. Adding you, Bennie, to the equation is what makes it a dream.

Note 70

I mourn past relationships, and I treasure existing relationships. I look forward to future relationships.

Note 71

I know I am capable of love. I know that I know how to love. I yearn to caress every aspect of my lover. I desire to be a living sanctuary,a resting place for him when life becomes too much to bear. I am looking for my King.

Note 72

Do I die because you tried to *kill* me, Bennie? Hell No!!

Note 73

I am left to ponder, how does one swallow bitterness? Does it go down better with sugar or honey? Do you take a big bite of it and swallow it whole without chewing? Do you chase it with a sweet liqueur? Do you grow a pair and eat the entire thing and then go about scowling and frowning from the bad taste in your mouth? Do you just leave it onthe plate and order another item from the menu:

Note 74

My life has been a series of ups and downs. The ups are so high that the earth was like a trinket or a shiny piece of jewelry. The downs are so low I can't see from beyond the grave. I live for each moment, whether up or down. I stand on my faith that downs will pass quickly, and the ups will linger forever. Living and loving is the duty of every human being. I am still a work in progress.

Note 75

Today, I choose me instead of you. I am better than you think I am. I have faith and high hopes for better days with someone who loves me. It's my choice not to hate. I will not allow myself to be bitter and turned into a scornful woman. I will continue to love with the intensity I showed you. I release all pain into the abyss. I pour love into the universe. I forgive everyone who hurt me today and forever. I choose to live. Love and I are one.

Note 76

He reached into my mind and healed my heart. He commanded me to come forth like Lazarus and live. He resuscitated my soul and helped me to breathe. He loved me with his life and captured my heart. His voice commanded me to respect myself. He gave me the strength to love again. His is the hand that I reach for when I stumble in the dark. He is my heavenly father. He is God!

Note 77

I gave myself to you wholeheartedly. I tried to belong to you, and you rejected all the broken pieces of me. I have a choice of how I react. If I choose to be bitter, acting the part of a woman scorned, you win. If I choose to thrive and show unconditional love, God wins. Today, I choose to belong to no man. Today, I choose *God*!

Note 78

To be halfhearted or perform halfheartedly in anything will not lead to success. You must love and live with your whole heart. That means loving with your entire being is crucial if you want your mind, body, and soul to survive.

Note 79

To master the art of love. You have to get to know love. You must define love; Recognize the characteristics of love; Acknowledge love is an emotion; Identify the target for love; Demonstrate love, and Repeat the above daily.

Note 80

Adverse experiences should not turn you against love. Relish it when you are in its presence. Crave it when it is absent. Above all, demonstrate it in all you do. It is the one true commandment from God.

Note 81

If I can give my all to a wretch like you, I know for sure that I can humbly submit to a righteous man. I can love and cherish a righteous man with my entire being. I can give my heart and body to a righteous husband. Loving a righteous man is my heart's desire. God loved me a thousand years before I was born. He is always there to guide me to the light. For that, I pledge my love only to God. I think I might get it right this lifetime.

Note 82

I think I hate you or do I hate me. How much I value myself has been brought into question. I have to relearn how to love myself. I call back the parts of me from all unworthy men. I am challenging myself to move forward in my life. Each day I will take steps moving toward the goal of reincarnating myself. I look forward to who I will become.

Note 83

People want to possess me sexually. They never hear my voice or anything I say. I am working on my approach with men. I monitor what I am putting into the universe? How do I command my respect? How do I turn off my sexy? Wait! Why do I have to? Maybe it is not my problem. God made me this way. I think I'll keep being my sexy self.

Note 84

My soul is set free from the burden of you. Free as the waves that thrash against the shore. Free as the breeze on a warm summer day. I am free to be myself again.

Note 85

Bennie, I no longer get a knot in the pit of my stomach when I think of you. The pain in my heart has subsided. The holes that you left in my life and my bank account have been filled and paved over. It was a bumpy ride, but I am wiser for it. I can only see smooth roads ahead. My journey to love is just beginning, and my future is brighter than before.

Note 86

My God has not forsaken me. I know there are angels encamped around me, protecting me and guarding my heart. Knowing God loves me gives me the strength to Love again.

Sirrah's Recovery

Sirrah prayed, cried, felt ashamed, felt guilty, wanted to kill Bennie, and wanted to kill herself. She mourned the life she had before Bennie. Her Notes were raw and spontaneous. About six months into her writing tantrum, Sirrah was fresh out of things to say about Bennie Zoudiki. She no longer wondered where he is or if that was his name. The idea of not being at the end of the alphabet made her smile. Had she married him, their children would always be last in line alphabetically. She never bothered to inquire or try to track him down. She decided it would be an act of futility. Her thoughts were no longer focused on Bennie.

Sirrah knew her drama was over when she noticed the beauty of a sunset for the first time. Her olfactory senses were also returning. Initially, the ordeal with Bennie left Sirrah so devastated that she couldn't smell her perfume. Now, her sense of smell was back. Flowers regained their beautiful aroma. Glancing in the mirror, she noted that her image was the same; it was her heart that changed. The golden flecks in her hair and the radiance of her bronze skin reminded Sirrah that shewas a goddess. It was her time to live again.

Sirrah initially wrote Notes to document her pain so that her family would have answers after she took her life. Her motivation had also changed. She decided to create a document outlining her emotional experience, thinking that her story might help someone. Also, she hoped that there was a slim chance that someone who knew the rat Bennie would turn him over to the authorities. Sirrah does not doubt that she was not the first woman Bennie Zoudiki conned and probably won't be the last.

Sirrah shared the agony and pain of unrequited love wanting others to know that they are not alone. She wanted it to serve as a warning to follow your inner voice. It takes time to get to know people. Ask questions about family, relationships, and criminal history. Be persistent about getting answers to those questions. Look beyond the physical appearance. Be ready to run away. Even then, there is a possibility that they may hurt or take advantage of you. Love is a gamble. Although it hurts to lose, the game is worth it.

Sirrah didn't give up on love. Her ordeal made her a believer. She learned that God's grace and Mercy will always prevail. When your gut and instincts are screaming foul, it is God trying to tell you no. Sirrah's family and teammates had misgivings about Bennie. Sirrah ignored all of the signs. It pays to value the opinion of the people that have your best interest at heart. Listening to your loved ones may save you from heartache. If everyone around you sees a rat, you shouldn't dress it up and call it handsome or pretty.

Epilogue

We set specific goals in our lives, and we are willing to work toward those goals. We tend to put those things before everything. Forsaking families and abandoning beliefs and morals, we live together out of wedlock. For most women, this goes against moral values and traditions. Through our hearts and the lust of our flesh, we convince ourselves that if we forsake ourselves that we will be made whole in the end. Sometimes we know that God is telling us, "No." We often pray and get our answer, whether in action or deed, but we choose to ignore all red flags. People can raise concerns about our beloved. We are afraid to bring up those issues because we don't want to know the truth. We end up paying dearly or overpaying for something that we should get upfront. The lover we work so hard for, and give so much of ourselves to, should love us enough to commit to us. They should love us enough to marry, build a life, and have a family with us. More importantly, we should love ourselves enough to walk away when we don't get what we want from the relationship. If our expectations don't get satisfied, it breaks our hearts. We blame the ex before we blame ourselves, then we get mad at love. If we carefully examine the situation, the warnings were probably there in the very beginning. It's our fault that we made the wrong choice when we decided to forsake everything for our partner's love. We have to learn how to forgive ourselves.

Love gets a bad rap because people willfully use it as a means to an end. The promise of love is offered as the prize for an act and used to barter for more love. An example of bartering is, "If you love me, you will do what I want, or I let you do this to show you that I love you." Sirrah sacrificed her virginity to prove to Bennie how much she loved him. It was against her moral values. He didn't appreciate what she gave him. Bennie selfishly wanted more. He demanded a baby.

The maddening consequences of a broken can lead to hatred and bitterness if you let it. Sirrah found peace through the writing of her pain. Now that her mind is clear of the debris of a broken heart. She is free. Everything she didn't get to express verbally, she wrote in her *Notes From A Broken Heart.* Let her story be a reminder that suicide or violence is never the answer. Traditionally, seeking help for mental health issues had a stigma associated with it. If we knew someone struggling with mental wellness, we would dare not inquire about their psychological well-being for fear of insulting them or experiencing retaliation from their loved ones.

Still, negative attitudes toward seeking counseling and therapy are problems in many communities. It causes people to struggle through traumatic events alone and in silence. In some situations, people don't recover because they don't have the proper coping skills. It is essential to develop a reliable support system where mental health information is confidential.

The following organizations provide services and information to stock your psychological health wellness toolbox.

- Mental Health America (www.mhanational.org)
- MentalHealth.gov (www.mentalhealth.gov)
- National Alliance on Mental Illness (www.nami.org)
- National Suicide Prevention Lifeline (https://suicidepreventionlifeline.org): 1-800-273-8255 or (in case of imminent emergencies) 911
- Nowmattersnow.org (www.nowmattersnow.org): Text HOMEto 741741 to connect with a crisis counselor.

We must strive to remove the stigma associated with mental health challenges that prevent people from seeking counseling and treatment. We can arm ourselves with information. If we learn what we can about psychological health and wellness, we could identify characteristics in friends and loved ones in need and advocate for those who cannot speak or do for themselves.

Through education, we can promote a tolerant and compassionate society for everyone. There is no normal for how to react to trauma. The key to recovery is identifying healthy ways to cope. There is no cookie-cutter survival method. We must love ourselves enough to seek help. Find out what works for us as individuals. Never give up on life and have faith in a brighter tomorrow

Personal Reflection

The following space is for personal Notes. No matter what you are going through, you matter. In this space, you can say what you need to say, good or bad. This area is judgment-free. Feel free to explore your private thoughts. All are encouraged to write their Notes. It just might save you from the lingering consequences of heartbreak or stop you from destroying someone else's mental stability or breaking a heart.

We all have a story or a situation that challenges our sanity. Some people sort through things through journaling and Note-taking. This space is for your Notes. Suppose there was an opportunity to address a person who caused pain in your life. Do you know what you will say? Now is the time to say what you need to say. Here is a space to write your notes.

PERSONAL NOTES

PERSONAL NOTES

Elaine Wills M.Ed.

PERSONAL NOTES

About the Author

Elaine Wills is the author of The Power of Gia: Evolution of S- Hero, which provides insight into the impact of childhood trauma on adults. She writes about issues that take people out of their comfort zone. Real-life situations that are not openly discussed and swept under the rug inspire many of her stories, including emotional abuse and mental health.

Elaine is a mother, grandmother, sister, friend, educator, and author, but above all, a woman of faith. Her stories give life and relevance to situations that impact the character's mental health and stability. Her books reflect her belief that no matter what challenges life brings, the faith of a mustard seed will pull you through. There is a ray of hope in every situation, although it may take a while to see it. You will survive.

Elaine earned a Bachelor of Science degree from the University of Detroit and a Master of Education degree from Wayne State University in Michigan. She is a certified peer support specialist with certificates in suicide prevention, domestic violence advocacy, and mental health first aid. She is passionate about guiding others through difficult situations. Writing from the perspective of different characters allows her to be transparent and open.

"Writing gives me the freedom to move through various traumatic situations without reliving the brutality of personal trauma." *Elaine Wills*

End!